MW00932585

THE
CITY

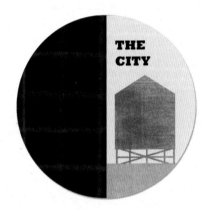

Bon

voyage

BUS

Dial Books for Young Readers
An imprint of Penguin Random House LLC, New York

Text copyright © 2019 by Jane Godwin
Illustrations copyright © 2019 by Blanca Gómez

Visit us online at penguinrandomhouse.com

Printed in China • ISBN 9780525553816
Design by Lily Malcom • Text set in Egyptian Slate Pro

10 9 8 7 6 5 4 3 2 1

For Trixie and Max, with love
—J.G.

To my friend Irene, a traveler mouse
—B.G.

For extra fun, look at the travel patches on the
endpapers. Can you match the picture in each
patch to its related image in the story?

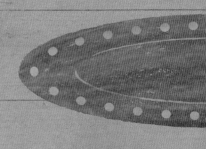

Red House Tree House
Little Bitty Brown Mouse

by Jane Godwin ★ illustrated by Blanca Gómez

Dial Books for Young Readers

Red house

Blue house

Green house

Tree house!

See the tiny mouse

in her little brown house?

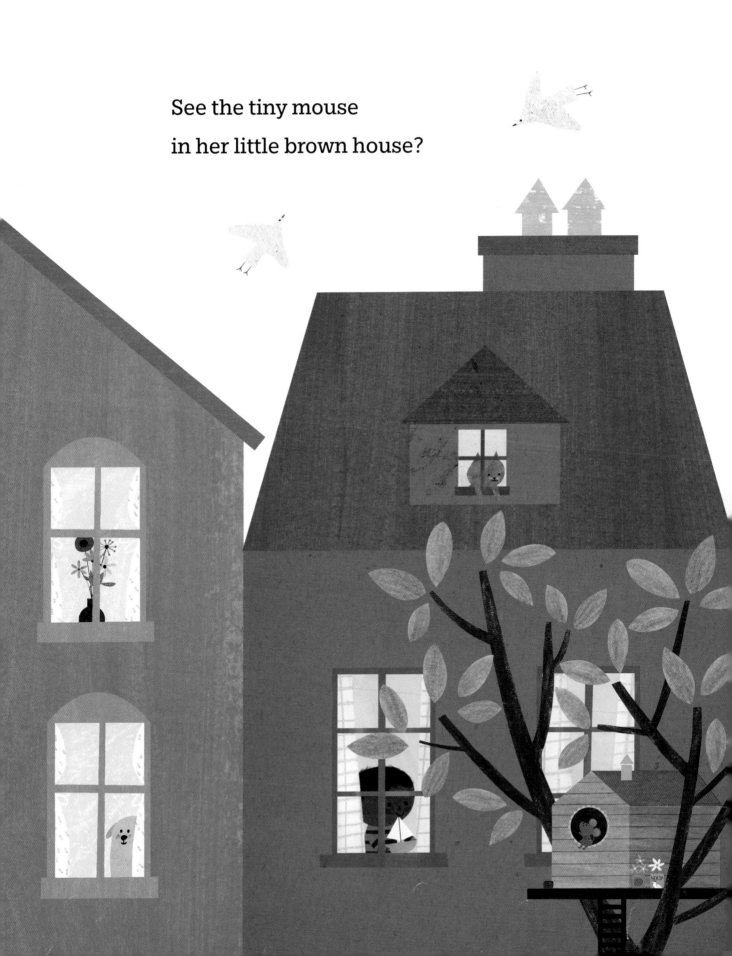

Blue flower
    Pink flower
Purple flower
    Red.

Can you count the petals
in the garden bed?

White rabbit

Gray rabbit

Black rabbit

Brown.

Floppy rabbit ears
going up and going down.

Yellow fruit

Pink fruit

Orange fruit

Green.

Do you know the color
of the berries in between?

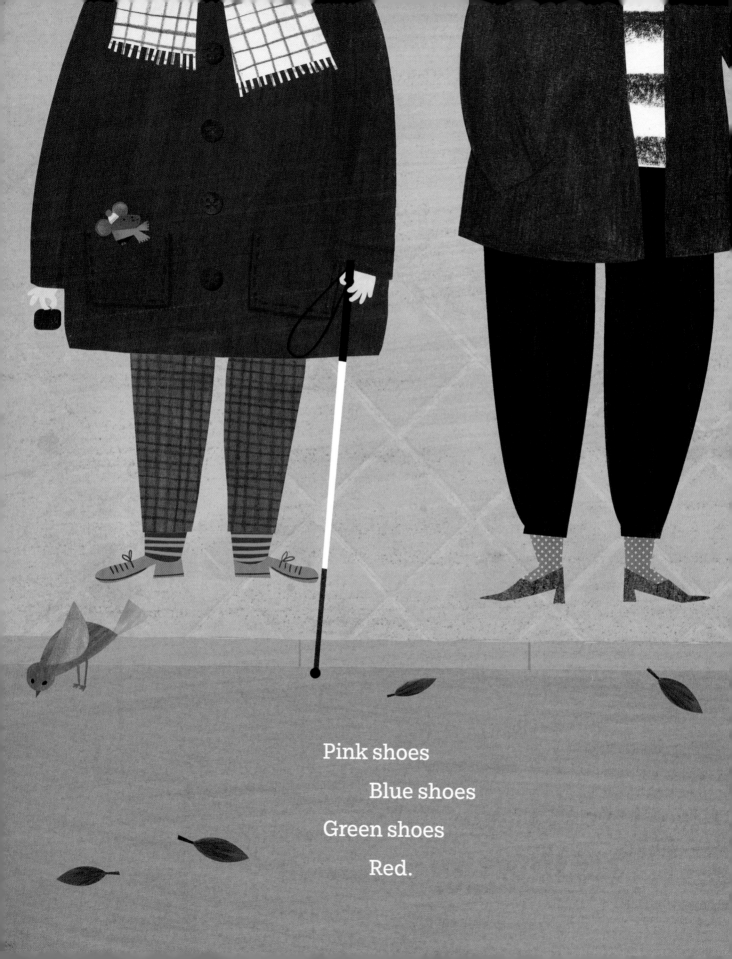

Pink shoes
Blue shoes
Green shoes
Red.

Shoes go on your feet.

What goes on your head?

Purple fish
Orange fish—
rainbow
tail.

Tiny darting silver fish . . .
one gigantic whale!

Ice cream
    that's smooth
And ice cream
    that's spotted.

Would you like the white one
or the one that's dotted?

Red boat

Yellow boat

Green boat

Pink.

Uh-oh . . .

Don't let that boat sink!

Orange bird
 Green bird
Gray bird's
   feather.

Watch the birds now,
flying all together.

Purple bike
Red bike
Scooter zooming
past.

Ding Ding

Beep Beep

W h e e !   That's fast!

Green train
    Red train
Speeding silver
    train.

See the trains sparkle
in the sun and in the rain?

Brown dog
Red dog
Dog with a
spot.

Dogs that are friendly,

and dogs that are not.

One, two,
      three balloons
gently floating
      by.

Drifting in the breeze,

and up into the sky.

Yellow sun
Silver rain
Clouds white and
gray.

See the rainbow colors
on a sunny rainy day?

Colors on a
sunny street—
what's your favorite
house?

Is it red or blue or green . . .

and did you spot that mouse?